OWEP

1234 HOPE

Chickens Don't Ski!

A Lily Saves the Day Book

Laura Willingham

The town of Blue Ridge was having its annual Winter Festival.
Lily was excited to attend because she lived far from town,
and she missed her friends.

As Lily and Dad made blueberry muffins and Mom packed the picnic basket it began snowing very heavily.

"We'll have to miss Winter Fest this year," stated Mom.
"We can't possibly make it on time walking in this snowstorm."

"There must be something we can do," fretted Lily.
"I really miss my friends," she sighed.

Lily searched all through the house looking for a solution.
Then she walked outside to the workshop.

She found six long pieces of wood. She used sandpaper to shape and smooth the edges and nailed thin ropes to the center of each piece. "Perfect!" she shouted.

Lily carried her creations into the house. "Look Mom and Dad! I made us skis! Now we can go to Winter Fest!"

"Chickens don't ski!" stated Mom.
"How do we know if we don't try?" Lily asked.

"It is downhill all the way to town.
We could get there very fast," Dad encouraged.
Dad reached for his backpack and
stuffed it full of picnic supplies and muffins.

After putting on their scarves, they went outside
and put on their skis.
"I'll go first," said Dad.
Dad took off down the hill.

He turned to the right.

He turned to the left.

He turned around and around but
when his skis slipped upwards,

he turned a backflip,

and landed headfirst in the snow!

"Oh no!" yelled Lily.
"We must help Dad!"
"I'll go," cautioned Mom.
"You stay here. It could be dangerous!"

Mom took off down the hill.

She turned to the right.

She turned to the left.

She turned around and around
but when she tried to slow down,

she fell over the front of her skis,

and landed headfirst in the snow!

"Oh no!" said Lily.
She could only see her parent's feet
and skis sticking out of the snow.
"I must help them!" she shouted.
"I'm coming to the rescue!"

Lily took off down the hill.

She turned to the right.

She turned to the left.

She turned around and around,
but then she skied over a small mound,

turned a cartwheel in midair,

and landed headfirst in the snow between Mom and Dad!

Being little, it was easy for Lily
to wiggle her way upright.
She shook herself off then
helped Mom and Dad out of the snow.

When they looked up, they realized
they were at the edge of town.

"We made it!" Dad yelled.

"Am I still alive?" Mom asked.

"You see, Mom! Chickens do ski!" Lily declared.

About the Author

Laura Willingham is a native of North Carolina. She is currently living on Monkey Island at Grand Lake in Oklahoma with her husband Barry and dog named Willie.

Her first book titled Chickens Don't Wear Tutus! was published in 2021. This story is about the same chicken family. Her purpose for writing and illustrating is to provide children with a moment of joy.

Outside of writing, she enjoys running, hiking, and spending time with family and friends.

Contact her and follow links: LauraWillingham.com

BLACK ROSE writing™

The final approval for this literary material is granted by the author.

First printing

This is a work of fiction. Names, characters, businesses, places, events and incidents are either the products of the author's imagination or used in a fictitious manner. Any resemblance to actual persons, living or dead, or actual events is purely coincidental.

ISBN: 978-1-68433-859-7 (Hardcover)
PUBLISHED BY BLACK ROSE WRITING
www.blackrosewriting.com

© 2021 by Laura Willingham

Printed in the United States of America

CPSIA information can be obtained
at www.ICGtesting.com
Printed in the USA
LVHW072100030322
712220LV00031B/557